# The

# Truth

## About

# Firefly

# Meadows

By: Olivia M. Sherry

Cover by Kaitlin Dolack

Illustrated by Ashlyn Warren


Special thanks to:

R.L. Stine, Jeff Kinney,
Mrs. Morgan, Janet Ivey, Judy
Pendleton, Barnes & Noble and to all
my family and fans who have helped
and supported me along the way.




www.oliviamsherry.com

# ✎Chapter One✐

April 13th, 1953, the night of the big storm.

Winds started up and dark clouds came into focus; thunder and lightning were crashing on top of each other and no more daylight could be seen at all. The small town of Phillipsburg would be hit the worst by this storm. Firefly Meadows, an old orphanage, was on the out-skirts of that town.

Kids and staff were scrambling and trying to get into the basement of the building.

"Is everyone here, are all of the children here?!" Madame Zoe asked in a panic.

The storm hit them so fast they did not have time to get everyone in an orderly way. One girl, Amanda Lakes, was not with the group of kids and staff members. That girl was on the roof of the orphanage, slowly backing up to the edge. A fall from the three-story building could easily hurt or kill someone.

"Stop, don't come any closer! Who are you?! Please, stop!!" Amanda screamed at someone who was up there with her, someone covered in a long, hooded raincoat closing in on her. The wind howled and the thunder echoed again. "No…no... NO!"

Lightning flashed as Amanda's body fell to the ground below.

# ✖Chapter Two✖

January 13th, 1955, the night of the fire.

Mr. and Mrs. Bleaster and their twelve-year old identical twins Anne and Bonnie lived in a modest home in Phillipsburg. One night, the stove had been left on by accident and caught a dishrag on fire. Soon the entire kitchen was in flames, then the whole house. The twins managed to escape but their parents' room was upstairs above the kitchen and they did not make it out in time. With no other relatives or family members that they knew of to care for them, the twins were now orphans.

Anne and Bonnie had nothing left except the nightgowns they were wearing that night.

Even though the sisters both have long, light brown hair and blue eyes, they are very different from each other. Anne has a bold personality and is good at solving things like puzzles and mysteries. For example; if Anne and Bonnie were trapped in a dark room, Anne would be the first to find the way out. She is good at finding clues (not surprisingly, her favorite book series is *Nancy Drew*).

Bonnie, on the other hand, is timid and shy. She mainly lets Anne lead the way for both of them. She was born two minutes before Bonnie after all.

It was two days after their parents were buried when Anne and Bonnie arrived at Firefly Meadows. All they had were some clothes and toiletries donated to them by a local church packed up in two suitcases.

It all happened too fast; Anne and Bonnie were still confused as to what has just happened these past three days (even though Bonnie is always confused) and the words were still ringing in their heads, *"You both will be going to Firefly Meadows Orphanage for girls and boys."*

They had been staying in a small motel with one of the staff members from Firefly Meadows, Ms. Maria. She was a very kind woman, tall and pretty with curly, black hair.

She helped out with everything the twins needed for their new lives.

The next day Anne and Bonnie found themselves in the backseat of a large car heading to their new home. Outside it was a crisp, cold day and the heat did not work in the car. The twins huddled together to stay warm. When they arrived, Anne stepped out of the car. Her hand me down coat swiftly blew in the wind. Bonnie followed her out in her tan coat. Both shivered in the breeze. Ms. Maria carried their suitcases.

A long pathway led to the gates of the orphanage. The building looked like an old castle, three floors of nothing but plain stone surrounded by a tall stone wall. They were way out in the country, Bonnie remembered that the last time they saw the town was miles ago. Old, bare, twisted trees led up to the orphanage with weeds all around dead grass. Long stretches of meadows filled the background, the wind was ghastly and rigid.

"It is so c-cold," Bonnie said shivering.

"I promise it will be warmer once we get inside," Ms. Maria said as she opened the big gates and let Bonnie and Anne in.

As they entered the building, Anne and Bonnie felt the warmth but also felt bewildered by what was going to be their new home. As they were looking around, they heard a woman's echoey voice say, "Hello, Ms. Maria," from down one of the hallways, "these must be the twin girls you told me about." It was Madame Zoe, the headmistress of the orphanage. She had long greyish blonde hair and was neatly dressed. She knelt down in front of the twin girls and said very sincerely, "I am so sorry for your loss, life can be very unfortunate. We here at Firefly Meadows want to make your stay as pleasant as possible while you wait to hopefully one day be adopted. Ms. Maria will put your belongings in your room, let me show you around."

She began giving them a tour saying, "This is the main building. In front of you under the staircase is the Dining Hall and a common room. There are three floors in each wing of this building, the one on the left is for the girls, the one on the right is for the boys." Madame Zoe led the girls up the main set of stairs in the middle of the building to the second floor. "This is the playroom complete with toys the younger boys and girls like to play with." The room was filled with dolls and rocking horses and was painted solid white. There were little tables with crayons and sheets of paper stacked on top of each other. "And over here is our library." The girls screeched with delight when they saw the small but full shelf of books.

"And over here is the school area for elementary grades. We will let you two get used to being here and living here before you begin your schooling." The room was full of desks and a big chalkboard, everything neat as a pin. "Soon you will meet with Mrs. Janet and Coach Curcio regarding your classes. Before you begin your lessons, you will have some pre-class work to do so we can make sure you are prepared." She smiled again, but then turned with a scowl and said, "There are areas around this facility that are off limits to all orphans, you may only go into the areas that I showed you at the specified times. If you don't, there will be consequences." Bonnie gulped with a frightened look on her face. "Now follow me back down."

As they walked back down the stairs, they saw a short, strange old man carrying some cleaning supplies coming up the stairs. "This is Mr. Claude, our janitor. He keeps things neat and clean around here," said Madame Zoe. Mr. Claude did not say anything but gave Anne a little sideways look…which gave her a weird feeling about him.

As they reached the bottom of the stairs, they turned to the back door outside of the dining area. There was the playground. Anne and Bonnie's eyes widened when they saw many kids playing out there.

"Well then, it's time you met the other children."

# ∽Chapter Three∾

Anne and Bonnie started walking towards the back door, they were both nervous and excited. As they went outside, they noticed that the sun was setting and the sky was splattered with orange, purple, and pink.

"Here we are," Madame Zoe said as she opened the door and showed the girls the kids playing on the playground. It didn't seem to matter how cold it was, the children were having fun.

Boys were playing basketball on the basketball court and girls were on the playground playing with toys. The ages of the orphans seemed to be from four years old to sixteen years old.

"Everyone!" Madame Zoe yelled as everyone stopped playing and looked her way.

"We have two new girls; their names are Anne and Bonnie Bleaster…as you can see, they are twin sisters. Please treat them nice and make them feel welcome." Anne looked at a boy on the field, he seemed rough. He had black hair and aqua blue eyes. He stared hard and mean at the twins. Bonnie gulped at the sight of him and tried to hide behind Anne who glared back at him.

"Well then, I am going to make sure your beds are ready in your room so you can just stay here and get to know the kids. If you need anything I will be back in my office." Madame Zoe walked back inside and left Anne and Bonnie outside with all the other kids who were starting to play again, ignoring the twins.

"Maybe we should try to make friends," Anne said. She noticed that a few of the boys kept on staring at them and they didn't look too happy.

Anne and Bonnie strolled through the playground with Bonnie shivering and Anne starting to see her breath. They saw some girls sitting at the swings and went over to them.

"Hello," Anne started.

The girls looked up from their conversation and one of them decided to talk, "Hey, um, we know you are new, and well, there might be some things you two would like to know; the food here is terrible and the teacher, Mrs. Janet, is pretty mean. She teaches a little of everything, mainly math." The girl then pointed over to the basketball court, "Those boys over there, they make a racket...and you see that guy with the black hair and that beat up coat?" Anne noticed that was the mean guy that was glaring at them a few minutes ago. "His name is Jason Brock. He is rude and will make your life pretty terrible if you mess with him."

The girl pointed to some other girls that were talking on a bench, "Those are the weirdos, they'll want nothing to do with you two. Oh, and that's Rose Bellards, the one in the wheelchair. She's paralyzed from the waist down. Thankfully, she can move her arms. Girls are assigned to help her with her daily needs, getting around, you know. Also, she can be a weirdo, too! One of my friends was taking care of her and said that she went to grab a toothbrush. When she came back Rose had crawled out of her wheelchair and disappeared for like half an hour before we found her in the corner of a room, crying. Anyway, never a dull moment around here I guess!"

"How does she get upstairs to her room?" Anne asked inquisitively.

"Oh, our P.E. teacher Coach Curcio carries her up and down the stairs, chair and all! She's pretty strong."

Then, another girl pointed to the monkey bars and said, "Those girls over there are pretty friendly. You can try to make friends with them, they might even be in your room! Now, about mealtimes. The boys will try to steal your food because they eat like hogs and they always want more than they need. Oh, and if you aren't careful when the staff isn't looking, they might throw rocks at you. I know from past experience..." All the girls behind her laughed. "Anyway, welcome to Firefly Meadows."

She turned around in her swing and started to talk to her friends again. Bonnie and Anne shivered and decided to go back inside to see the library and read some books. The cold was getting to be too much for them anyway.

When they got to the bookshelf, they noticed that almost all of the books were torn, some with missing pages. Most likely they were donated after about one hundred kids had already read them. Bonnie almost started crying and Anne was a little bit shocked.

"This is *not* fair," Anne grunted, flipping through book after book. Suddenly, some books on the bottom shelf caught Anne's eye.

"NO! It can't be!!" Anne excitedly yelled.

"What, WHAT?!" Bonnie asked.

"The *Nancy Drew* series!" She looked through a few of the books as her excitement turned to sadness when she found that they were so damaged she couldn't even read them. "They're all ruined!" Bonnie said. She felt so bad that she started crying on Anne's shoulder as Anne sighed.

"Do you think we should complain?" Bonnie asked.

Anne put away the books and shook her head, "No. What good would that do?"

When the girls headed out of the library and into the hallway, they could hear kids coming back inside. "Well," Anne said with another sigh, "we might as well explore our new home."

Bonnie and Anne peeked inside most of the rooms. Nothing too interesting; they just looked like old bedrooms. They saw one with an old wheelchair in it. Maybe in case another child needed one.

Just about every room was mostly empty, then they got to the last room in the hall. Anne tried to open the door but it was locked. "I guess we can't go in there," said Bonnie. Anne knew she probably shouldn't try to pick the lock, but she knows how to do that. She loves solving a good mystery and the temptation to find out what was in this room became too much. She took a pin from her hair and picked the lock. She slowly opened the door and saw...nothing, just another bedroom. But there was something unusual. The floor and the walls were scratched up, like with fingernails. The claw marks made the wallpaper hang off the wall like long leaves. Anne and Bonnie stared intently when all of a sudden, the door was thrown open wide.

"Girls!" Madame Zoe shrieked at the doorway, "How did you get in here?! You're not allowed in this area! Get back downstairs at once!!"

As they went downstairs, Madame Zoe continued, "As I told you already, we have strict rules around here and they must be followed or there WILL be consequences!" Just then a scream came from outside. Ms. Maria ran in the front door and yelled up to Madame Zoe, "Get help!!"

"What is it?!"

"One of the boys was found in the woods. He is soaking wet and freezing to death! Call an ambulance!"

# ∽Chapter Four∾

"What is his full name?" Police Officer Clark asked.

"Johnson, Henry Johnson," Madame Zoe said as she watched the boy being placed into an ambulance.

Officer Clark scratched his neck, "Well, we don't have much information and he isn't talking. It appears he wasn't being looked after and nearly drowned in a pond out in the meadow." Officer Clark looked up at the orphanage and made a strange face, "You know, this kind of thing doesn't need to happen any more than it already—"

"Yes, I understand Officer Clark," Madame Zoe interrupted so the children wouldn't hear the rest of what he might say, "I'll be in touch if I find anything else out that might help explain what happened." The officers got back in their car and drove off with the ambulance.

Zoe turned to the kids, "Well, everyone, what happened with Henry Johnson was an unfortunate accident. He knew that no children are allowed outside of the gates of the orphanage! This needs to be a lesson for all of you. Now, it's time for dinner!" Everyone was silent and followed her into the Dining Hall.

Anne and Bonnie were in line to get dinner. A kid was standing in front of them who seemed to be thirteen or so. Anne tapped his shoulder and asked, "What happened with that Henry kid?" The boy turned to them and said, "He decided to be stupid and go throw himself in a pond in the middle of winter. Not the best way to try to escape Firefly Meadows. Not the first time something like that has happened here you know."

The twins' eyes widened when they heard what he said. Anne was just about to ask the boy something else when he left the line and they were handed their trays. The dinner was soup, stale bread, grapes and corn on the cob. Bonnie beamed with delight at the sight of the bread, but when she looked at the corn, she made a sour face. It had yellow juice squirting out of every place it shouldn't. She would not be eating the corn.

Finally, Anne and Bonnie got out of the dinner line and headed toward the rows of kids at the old, wooden tables. They noticed boys stealing food from the girls and gobbling it down as fast as they could. Bonnie and Anne sat down and started eating the salty soup, stale bread and the sour, mushy grapes.

"I wonder what that boy was talking about?" Bonnie asked slowly crunching her stale bread.

Anne sighed and looked down at her food shaking her head, "I don't know Bonnie, but I want to find out."

It was eight o' clock and everyone was getting ready to go to bed. Bonnie and Anne looked around the orphanage to find their room when they saw the girls that they met a few hours ago.

"Hi," Anne said to the one girl with blonde, curly hair.

"Looking for your room, I presume?" the girl asked.

"Well, yeah," Anne said.

"The girls' wing is over here, follow me."

Lights were starting to go out which made the hallway quite creepy. Bonnie tried to hold Anne's hand, almost. It seemed to be as long as a city block, but finally they were at their room. The blonde girl led them inside where seven neatly made up beds were all next to each other. Across from them were two dressers, a changing curtain, and a door to a bathroom. It was a pretty small room with two huge windows and plain white walls. It wasn't much, but it was better than nothing. On the wall was a list of several girls' full names who occupied the room.

"Well, here are your cots. Breakfast is at 6am, lunch is at 12pm, and dinner is at 5:30pm. Wake up before 5am so you can make up your cot and get dressed. I had to learn that the hard way, the Madame does *not* like late sleepers. If she finds you asleep after five o'clock you will be in a world of trouble!"

"Well you already know that I'm Anne Bleaster and this is my twin sister Bonnie, but what are your names?"

"I'm Reagan," said the girl with long, thick, red hair that you could tell must get brushed a lot, "you and your sister are in this room with Maddie, Caitlyn, Ruby, Louise, Judy, and…"

"ROSE!!!" A girl screamed outside the door interrupting Reagan. She stormed into the room pushing Rose in her wheelchair. She was a bigger girl, not fat but large and strong looking.

"I TOLD YOU NOT TO GO ANYWHERE WITHOUT ME! QUIT TRYING TO ROLL OFF!" They both stopped in their tracks surprised to see the girls standing there.

Reagan rolled her eyes and continued, "These two are Rose and Louise. Louise is helping Rose this week." Anne looked at Rose. Her long, brown hair almost completely covered her timid face. Anne and Bonnie remembered that Rose was paralyzed from the waist down…poor girl!

"Hi, Rose, I'm Anne and this is Bonnie," Anne said to Rose who was silent.

"I forgot to mention that Rose is *very* shy and she really doesn't like to talk to anyone, case closed."

Louise pushed Rose to the other side of the bedroom to help her get ready to go to bed.

Reagan said goodbye and left the room, Anne and Bonnie decided to get ready for bed also.

It was pitch black after Anne and Bonnie finished getting dressed for bed. Their eyes adjusted to the darkness and they climbed into their beds that were next to each other. They noticed that two of the girls were snoring, loudly. Another girl was running in her sleep and the others were in weird positions as they lay in their beds.

By midnight, Anne was asleep, snoring. Bonnie was still wide awake. She looked around and thought, *I wonder when Mommy and Daddy will come get us?*

It was early morning when Anne and Bonnie woke up. They noticed that everyone else was still sleeping. So, they quietly slipped into some of their donated clothes and walked out of their room. There was a long hallway that connected the wing to the rest of the orphanage lined with old stained-glass windows that were almost completely opaque.

"Anne, are we lost?" Bonnie looked around, frightened.

"No, we're just turned around and need to figure out how to get down to the Dining Hall."

Anne and Bonnie started to walk farther and farther, getting more and more lost as they went on.

"Anne?"

"What is it, Bonnie?"

"Are we lost now?"

"Bonnie!" Anne glared at her and Bonnie knew to keep her mouth shut. Then a look came over Bonnie's face as she walked towards a staircase like she was in a trance.

*"Follow me..."* a voice said from the hallway.

Bonnie looked around, "Who said that?"

"Said what?" Anne asked.

Bonnie started to run. Anne ran after her.

"Bonnie, where are you going? I don't think the Dining Hall is down that way!"

They raced down a staircase around a corner. Barely keeping up, Anne tried to stop Bonnie in her tracks, but Bonnie seemed to be following something.

All of a sudden, she stopped in front of the door of the locked room they got in trouble for being in the day before. The room that had scratch marks on the floor and wall. Anne shuddered looking at it and tried to push Bonnie away from the door. Suddenly, the door opened by itself like it was welcoming them in. Both girls were somehow pulled inside and the door shut behind them.

Anne got up and tried to open the door, but it was locked. Bonnie was passed out on the floor.

"Bonnie! Please answer me!" Anne shook Bonnie until she woke up.

Bonnie shook her head and said, "Hey, how did we get here?"

"You don't know?" Anne looked astonished as her sister looked around in fright.

"What did I do?" Bonnie looked at the clawed wallpaper and became upset.

"You didn't do anything, but I think we are locked in. Madame Zoe is going to be so angry at us...again!"

# ↬Chapter Five↫

"Bonnie stop!" said Anne to her sister who had been banging on the door for the past five minutes.

"Bonnie, it's no use. I don't think anyone can hear us from in here; but I think we could get out by climbing out that window." Anne tried to open the room's only window which showed the grey, dull, sunless sky…but it was stuck. Bonnie started to panic.

"Calm down Bonnie, we can use something to pry it open. Look for some kind of bar or tool!"

Anne started looking in the wardrobe that was in the corner of the room near the door. She pulled hard to open the doors…nothing but cobwebs.

"Anne I'm scared," Bonnie started to panic again, but Anne stopped her.

"You go look over there in the nightstand drawer and see if you can find anything that will help us get out of here," Anne said with a worried expression on her face.

Bonnie patted Anne's back.

"Don't worry, sis, everything will be all right when Mommy and Daddy pick us up soon!"

Anne became frustrated with Bonnie but didn't want to explain then and there that she was fooling herself.

Anne stood up straight and got into *detective mode*. "So, there are fingernail scratch marks on the wall which means someone was trapped in here before. But scratching the wallpaper is not a way out. Hmmm."

"We have to get out of here, Anne."

"I know Bonnie!" Anne started digging around underneath the mattress until she felt a slip of paper. She carefully pulled it out and read it:

July 6, 1944

I know I am probably not going to survive this place much longer, and I feel like they will use me again. Their procedures may end my life. If that happens and you want to try to find out why, don't. You will risk your life.

*I love you sweetie, from the bottom of my heart. I am so sorry I wasn't there for you, I wanted to be a good father to you. All I can tell you is that whatever you do, never go to Firefly Meadows. There is danger in this place, especially in the basement. That is where they conduct e.x-*

"I can't read the rest of it, it's rotted away. But whoever wrote this letter must have been locked in this room."

Bonnie came over and looked over Anne's shoulder. When she finished reading, she looked at Anne with her eyes filled with fear.

"I just realized something," Bonnie said in a shaky voice.

"What? What did you just realize?"

"His handwriting…" Bonnie looked back down with tears filling her eyes, "is better than *my* handwriting!!" Bonnie started to cry.

Anne looked at her and rolled her eyes, "Bonnie, *CALM... DOWN!!* We have been through much worse than this! You *have* to stop crying!"

But Bonnie couldn't stop crying. Pretty soon Anne started feeling overwhelmed by everything too. She started jumping up and down, letting out all of her anger and stress, wishing her parents were there to calm them both. To take them home. Bonnie joined in jumping too. The sisters jumped and jumped and *jumped*. It was a few minutes later when they heard footsteps coming up the stairs to the hallway…and then the opening of the door. Outside in the hallway stood Mr. Claude with an angry look on his face holding a set of keys that were swinging in his hand.

# ∽Chapter Six∾

Anne and Bonnie had massive headaches the next day. Since it was their second time getting in trouble for the *same thing*, they both got cleaning duty for a whole week by Madame Zoe. It was a nasty task; they had to clean just about everywhere in the orphanage (even the boys' wing!)

The next day they began their cleaning duties, no schooling yet, just work.

"Hey, um… Anne?" Bonnie came shuffling over the wet classroom floor they had been scrubbing for half an hour, "Is it time for lunch yet?"

Anne was on her hands and knees in a big room with five windows showing the endless gray sky that hadn't changed in days.

"Um, I think in another two hours Bonnie."

"How do you know that for sure?" Bonnie crossed her arms, her stomach growling.

"Bonnie don't start—"

"I NEED FOOD!! If I don't have food, I won't be able to clean the floors, or clean the windows, or make the beds, or—"

"OK! You want food so you can continue doing this dreadful work, I get it…but it's going to be a while until lunch and I don't want us to get in any more trouble than we're already in."

Bonnie sighed, "We can slip into the pantry, find some of that *yummy* stale bread and *then* scrub the rest of the floor."

Anne stared hard at Bonnie, "OK fine, go look for stale bread, or whatever. It's your funeral."

Anne went back scrubbing the floor again.

Bonnie rolled her eyes, opened the door and walked out of the room, out in the hallway and slowly walked down the stairs into the Dining Hall.

There were three doors next to the lunch line area. She remembered which one was the kitchen. The last one was Ms. Maria's office. The third one must be the pantry!! Bonnie tried to open it. It was locked.

Before Bonnie began to cry again, the door unlocked itself and opened revealing a staircase. *Hey! This might be the pantry!* Bonnie thought.

Bonnie started to walk down the steps. She put her hand on the wall as she stepped further down until she couldn't feel the wall anymore and stepped onto the floor.

"Hello? Stale bread? Where are you?" Bonnie could still see the door and the light from the Dining Hall clearly, but everything else was hidden by darkness.

Bonnie was starting to think that this was not a pantry at all when out of nowhere a lightbulb hanging from the ceiling flickered, lighting the room for a few split seconds. All she could see were empty, dusty shelves and several wooden boxes stacked up against the back wall. The stairs were the only way in or out. Then Bonnie felt as if she was being watched. She looked around, feeling her way through the room as the light continued to flicker on and off like a slow strobe light. Bonnie wasn't scared. When she heard the clock upstairs strike eleven, she knew that lunch would be in an hour. The light went out again and total darkness resumed.

*Might as well wait until lunchtime now,* Bonnie thought as she found her way back to the staircase and started walking up. She smiled as she smelled the green pea soup that was cooking. But before she reached the top, the door closed by itself.

Bonnie stopped in her tracks as the light started flickering off and on again.

"Who is doing this to me?" she asked nervously, looking around the room.

*"Come down here..."* said a voice that sounded like a young girl.

"Why?" Bonnie whispered.

*"I need to show you something,"* the voice said.

"Is it where they keep the stale bread?"

Bonnie felt her way back down the steps, her heart beating fast. She put her hands on the wall and started feeling to the corner of the room. As she got closer to the corner, she noticed the room getting colder and colder.

"Where are you?" Bonnie asked as she felt along the cold wall of the room.

"*Over here...*" The girl's voice sounded like she was right next to Bonnie.

The flickering light went completely out and Bonnie froze. Suddenly, the light came fully on and a girl was standing right in front of her! Bonnie gasped. The girl was wearing a dirty nightgown and her long, brown hair was tangled and windblown. Bonnie started talking to her, "Oh, we haven't met yet, I'm Bonnie Bleaster. My twin sister Anne and I are here for a little while until our parents come to pick us up. What is it you want to show me?"

The girl pointed to an open doorway right next to her. A doorway that wasn't there before.

*How did that get there?* Bonnie thought.

A bright light came from the inside of the door. Bonnie covered her eyes as the light got brighter and brighter and brighter.

Soon she could see an outside scene through the doorway. She walked through the door into bright daylight. She was outside in a forest; the sun was out and no clouds were in the sky. As she looked around, she overheard voices not too far away from where she was. Bonnie started walking in the direction of the voices, then she stopped in her tracks. Standing before her was the orphanage. She was in the woods outside the gates of Firefly Meadows! The building was the same, except it looked newer. Bonnie then noticed that there were two men in front of the gates. She slipped behind a tree and eavesdropped on their conversation.

"It really does match the blueprints, Jackson," one of the two men said, "You really aren't lying when you say you can build anything once you put it on paper."

"Thank you, Aiden," the other man said.

"Now, what is this building going to be used for anyways?"

"Oh, get this, it's going to be an insane asylum!"

Then, just like that, Bonnie was lying on the floor of the dark basement, confused about what she had just seen. And still hungry.

# ∾Chapter Seven∾

Bonnie was still trying to understand what was going through her head after hearing those words. An insane asylum? This place? What's an insane asylum? Bonnie looked around. The door to the outside had disappeared and so did the girl she was talking to. Suddenly the door at the top of the stairs opened again.

"Hello? Bonnie, are you down there?" someone whispered at the top of the stairs.

"Anne? Yeah, I'm down here."

"Get back up here now. I'm sure you're not supposed to be down there and we're going to get in trouble again…is that a basement?!"

Bonnie started to feel her way up the stairs to the Dining Hall.

"Bonnie! Hurry! Everyone else will be here in less than a minute!"

Bonnie rushed up every creaky step. She must have been passed out for a while! Finally, she made it to the top and Anne quickly but quietly shut the door behind her. Right then the other orphans started filing in.

Anne and Bonnie got in line for lunch, watching Mr. Claude mop the floor. His gray hair looked messy and seemed to have not been washed in a few weeks. His long nose hung out over his brown mustache as he snarled at the orphans. He then grabbed his bucket of water and walked up the stairs.

"What's his problem?" Bonnie asked.

"I don't know," Anne muttered, "maybe he just doesn't like to mop floors in a creepy orphanage all the time. Or maybe he just doesn't like kids…or both."

Anne and Bonnie were handed lunch trays and the lunch lady, Barbra, served up some split pea soup (which looked awful) and handed the girls a couple of pieces of stale bread. Bonnie was giddy with excitement.

"I've been waiting a long time for this bread, it's like heaven for me. Thank you, Ms. Lunch Lady. I just feel so tingly inside when I take a bite—"

"Will you just move along, kid?" Barbra snarled as she pulled her hair net down over the warts on her forehead, "There are lots of kids in line and you just want to make fun of the bread!"

"Oh no, she's serious," said Anne, "She loves stale bread more than fresh bread. Her favorite snack when she was little was croutons. I don't get it either." Bonnie nodded her head.

"Whatever you say," Barbra looked at the line of kids waiting for their meals, "Next!"

Anne and Bonnie went to get their water, sat down and tried to start eating.

"Bonnie, how did you get down to the basement and how could you stay down there that long?"

Bonnie was already crunching into her stale bread as crumbs began flying everywhere.

"Bonnie," Anne looked hard at her, "BONNIE!"

"What?"

"Why did you go into the basement? You remember what that letter that we found said!

And how did you end up staying down there for like an hour?!"

"That was the basement?"

Anne rolled her eyes as she said, "Yes!"

"What? I thought that was the pantry there because of the girl that lives in there," Bonnie said through another mouthful of bread.

"There was a girl down there? What are you talking about? Madame Zoe said that we are not allowed in the basement! How could anyone be living down there? You must be seeing things, Bonnie."

"Well she was the one that showed me the door to the outside."

"Bonnie, there shouldn't be any door to the outside in the basement, the basement is underground…that wouldn't make any sense!"

"Well that is true, after I went back through the door it disappeared."

"Bonnie, you are crazy!" Anne rolled her eyes *again* and started eating her lunch.

After lunch, everyone went to P.E. class except for Anne and Bonnie…they had to do more chores. They started cleaning the rooms upstairs. Each one seemed dirtier than the next.

"Ew!" Anne said as she picked up used tissue. "Does the janitor do anything around here?"

Bonnie was across the room wiping the window, looking at all of the kids outside running around the meadow. "Are you sure we're supposed to clean these rooms?"

"Well, when Madame Zoe said to clean all of the rooms, she didn't say to not clean these! Besides, the punishment is over in a few more days."

"Well, if you say so…" Bonnie started wiping the window again and Anne started to sweep the floor.

Night rose from the hills outside of the orphanage. Anne and Bonnie finished cleaning all of the rooms on the second floor (except the last one on the left where Anne and Bonnie had gotten in trouble).

As they collected all of the supplies they used, Anne wiped the sweat off her forehead.

"At least we can go to sleep in beds. Madame Zoe almost decided that we should sleep on the floor!" Anne said.

"What? She did?"

Anne shook her head as they headed towards the stairs.

"There you two are!" Sydney said as she and Ruby rushed up to Anne and Bonnie, "We have been looking everywhere for you two! Where have you been?"

"We still have to do our punishment," Anne started.

"Cleaning this place takes a lot of time!" Bonnie finished.

"Oh, I remember those kinds of punishments," Sydney said laughing, "two months ago I accidentally…"

"Sydney!" Ruby said widening her eyes.

"Okay, okay! Two months ago, during recess, I *purposely* kicked a soccer ball at Jason, and it *kind of* broke his nose, and he *kind of* fell into a ditch, and he *kind of* sprained his ankle."

"Well if you ask me, he probably deserved it," Anne said.

They all looked at Jason where he was standing in the common room with some of his friends. When he noticed we were looking at him (especially Sydney) he sneered then looked away fast.

All the girls laughed. But when Anne, Sydney, and Ruby stopped laughing, Bonnie was on the ground rolling around and laughing very hard. Everyone down in the common room and on the stairs stopped and looked at Bonnie, the room was silent besides the loud laughter. Finally, she noticed how everyone was staring at her, so she got back up, gazing blankly at the wall.

Anne was red faced with embarrassment, but cleared her throat and said to Sydney and Ruby, "Well, see you two later."

"Yeah, bye."

Anne pulled Bonnie down the stairs and outside as the voices from the room and Dining Hall faded a little.

"Bonnie what were you doing in there?! You completely embarrassed me, and in front of everyone! What were you thinking?"

Bonnie stared blankly at Anne, "I thought it was funny, you were all laughing!"

"It wasn't THAT funny! What is it, Bonnie? You have been weirder than usual the last few days. I can tell that something is up with you! Are you hiding something from me?"

Bonnie's eyes filled with tears. She rushed back into the building and shut the door in Anne's face. But as she looked around, everyone in the Dining Hall and common room were now gone, the lights were out and all Bonnie could make out were the empty tables in the moonlight.

"Hello? Where did everyone go? Come on, this is not funny!" Bonnie said. No one came out; everyone was gone.

"Anne! What happened?" Bonnie turned around to look for her sister, but there was no one there.

Slowly the basement door began to open and out walked the girl from earlier.

"Hi again," the girl walked close to Bonnie.

"What is your name?" asked Bonnie.

"Amanda, Amanda Lakes."

"Mine is Bonnie, where is everyone?"

"They are… gone right now. Anyway, you have to follow me, please. I don't have much time before—" Amanda started shaking in fear.

"Before what?" Bonnie looked confused.

"Before he finds out I am helping you!" The words spilled out. Amanda covered her mouth with her gray hands.

"Who?"

Amanda took a deep breath, "There is something you need to know. You have a very special gift. This is the ghost world you are in and you are able to see it."

"Ghost world?! You mean…you're a ghost? I thought you were just another orphan here."

"I was. I am the girl who died falling off the roof of this building two years ago. What people don't know is that I was PUSHED off! I don't know who did it because there was a horrible storm that night and whoever it was had a large raincoat on that covered their face."

"What do you want from me?" asked Bonnie nervously.

"There is a very bad ghost in this orphanage. This spirit is responsible for killing me and hurting the other children here. Do you remember what you saw when you were in the basement?"

"When I was outside?"

"Yes! Now do you remember what you saw?"

"Well, yes. I saw two men, and the orphanage looked new."

"Bonnie, this wasn't originally an orphanage!! This was an insane asylum!"

"That's what one of the men said. What is that?"

"It is a place where crazy people are locked up. Sometimes they are not treated well and sometimes they die in very bad ways. Look, before he finds me let me just tell you this, those injuries to the orphans aren't on accident, they are on purpose."

As soon as Amanda said those words, Bonnie noticed everything started to spin around in circles, faster and faster.

"Wait, who is it that is doing these things?" yelled Bonnie, "What is happening around here?!"

But Amanda was gone and everything was dark. Then Bonnie saw a big light in the distance. The light became brighter and brighter, closer and closer until it surrounded her and she was back in the Dining Hall again, the real one with everyone there eating.

"What? How?" Bonnie asked herself.

"Bonnie!" Anne came running over. "I am so sorry. I didn't mean to make you cry."

"It's okay," Bonnie said softly.

Then they heard a horrible coughing sound. They looked over at one of the boys who was at his table, his face turning pale. He was starting to choke. Suddenly, foam started coming out of his mouth! The orphans started to scream and didn't know what to do. Ms. Maria heard the noise and ran out of her office.

"Oh my! I think he's been poisoned! Everybody, stop eating what you're eating!!"

Ms. Maria and all of the staff did what they could to help the poor boy and an ambulance was called. All of the orphans were looking around at each other, suspecting each and everyone but themselves.

Bonnie was still confused by everything that had been happening to her. Anne was busy looking at the faces of everyone in the Dining Hall from Mr. Claude, who was helping take the boy outside, to Rose, who was sitting in her wheelchair staring down at her food.

# ✂Chapter Eight✂

"Madame Zoe, you know I can't keep coming back here over and over again to investigate when your orphans keep dying or disappearing or getting hurt at your facility. The state will shut you down if this keeps happening!" said Officer Clark. He was with several other policemen as the ambulance drove off with the poisoned boy.

"I know, Officer Clark," said Madame Zoe, "I'm so, so sorry. It's just been a series of unfortunate accidents. We will handle everything better from now on."

Soon the police left Firefly Meadows, Madame Zoe and Ms. Maria walked back inside together. Officer Clark took one look back at the building before he got in his car and drove off.

It was after dinner when Anne and Bonnie and all of their roommates were racing each other down the hallways in their thirty minutes of free time. Usually Judy won, shoving anyone that got in front of her. Coming in last place would be Bonnie who has no idea how to run fast because she usually trips or stumbles.

After the break, all the girls started to walk to their room. It was dark outside and the moon was a hazy crescent barely showing through the cloud cover.

Anne walked up to Reagan and asked, "Why is this place called Firefly Meadows anyway?"

Reagan pointed outside the window to the darkened meadows and said, "Well, you can't tell now because it's winter, but out there in the spring and summer the meadows are filled with fireflies. Thousands of them. On a clear night you can't tell the difference between the fireflies and the stars. It's very pretty to see. Madame Zoe even lets us catch them sometimes before bedtime."

"I bet she won't even let us outside after dark because she's too afraid that one of us might have an 'accident' and wind up dead!" said Louise.

"Hey," said Anne, "what else has been going on around here besides…Henry and the kid who got poisoned, who else has been hurt?"

"Or killed," stated Maddie.

"Really?" asked Anne.

Caitlyn took a deep breath, "There was a girl here named Amanda Lakes. It was during a stormy night a few years ago that she jumped off the roof of Firefly Meadows. No one knew why, she didn't leave a note or anything. She died. After that we had a girl fall down the stairs and break her arm, and one boy who just…disappeared. One day he was here and the next he was gone!"

Everyone sat silently until Bonnie blurted,

"I know an Amanda!"

"Sure, you do," said Anne, "Caitlyn, do you really think that all of those events were accidents or do you think someone is responsible?"

"The girl who fell down the stairs said that she was pushed, but that the person who pushed her was wearing a hooded raincoat and it was at night so she couldn't tell who it was. Madame Zoe didn't even believe her story."

"Do you? Do you believe there's someone behind all this?"

"I don't want to talk about this anymore," yelled Louise, "let's just call it a night!"

As the girls were getting ready for bed, Anne had an idea about how to take everyone's mind off the subject they were talking about.

"Do you girls like riddles?" she asked.

A few moments later the girls were sitting in a circle in the center of the room. All of them were trying to remember a riddle they had heard. All except Rose who was in the corner of the room staring at the moon outside.

"Can I go first?" Anne asked.

"Does it look like we will stop you?" Judy huffed as she looked at the ceiling.

"Okay, well there is one riddle that is my favorite. So, Jennifer was the owner of a popular candy shop. One day the police found her strangled to death. She was holding two lollipops in her hand; one was blue and the other was yellow. There were no witnesses, but there were three suspects; Mr. Burnett, Ms. Green and Mrs. Stiles. Mr. Burnett said that he was at the barber shop across the street at the time of the murder, Ms. Green said she was driving her car to the store, and Mrs. Stiles, Jennifer's best friend, said she was next door buying some records. One of them was lying, who was it?"

All of the girls thought for a few minutes. Anne held her head up high as they all fumbled to come up with an answer.

"Oh! That is simple!" Bonnie self-confidently said as she stood up, "It was Mr. Burnett! Because he's probably old and bald and if he's bald it would only take a minute to get his hair cut. *SO* that means he had plenty of time to go to the sweets shop and kill the candy lady!"

"Bonnie," Maddie shook her head, "just sit back down."

Bonnie sat down next to Anne with a scowl on her face.

"So, will anyone else try to guess?" Anne smirked at everyone in the circle.

Everyone looked at each other, but no one said anything.

"Ha! Well, anyway, the answer is—"

"I know," said Rose.

Everyone turned their heads to the corner of the room where Rose sat there looking at the girls.

"Do you think you know, Rose?" Ruby asked.

"Well, I think it would be Ms. Green, because yellow and blue make green. The lollipops were yellow and blue..."

Everyone looked at Rose wide-eyed.

"Well, yes, that is correct," Anne said as she watched Rose make a little smile.

"I think it is time for bed now," Rose said in a hushed voice.

"Um, OK, Rose. I'll help you get into bed now," Louise said as she got up and pushed Rose over to her bed, picked her up out of her wheelchair and carefully put her into her bed. All of the other girls started going to bed too.

"Well, goodnight everyone," Maddie said.

"Goodnight!" all of the other girls said. Caitlyn flipped the light switch off.

The next day, Anne and Bonnie were in Madame Zoe's office. Their week of punishment was finally over.

"Now," Madame Zoe said as she got up from her desk and walked to a file cabinet, "everyone's records are in here." She opened one of the drawers and pulled out Anne and Bonnie's file folder. "You must understand that disobeying rules is not tolerated here and I really should put this on your records…"

Anne and Bonnie looked down at their feet.

"But I have a feeling you two learned your lesson and I feel like you two are good kids. So, I won't."

Anne and Bonnie sighed in relief.

"But!"

Anne and Bonnie jumped in their chairs.

"The next time you two disobey, it *will* go on your permanent records!" Madame Zoe put Anne and Bonnie's file folder back in the drawer and closed it shut. "Now that your punishment is over, you both can now participate in our school...and you have class with Mrs. Janet in five minutes, so go grab your books and get going!" Madame Zoe pulled open the door and led Anne and Bonnie out.

"If you have any questions, come to me!" Madame Zoe shut the door and left Anne and Bonnie in the hallway.

"Well, at least we don't have to scrub any more floors," Anne said.

"I guess," Bonnie looked down like she was going to cry.

"What is it Bonnie?"

"I—I,"

"Yes?" Anne waited.

"I don't want to go to school!" Bonnie started to cry.

"Don't cry, Bonnie! It won't be that bad!"

"Yes. It. Will. Be! Mrs. Janet is supposed to be tough and will give out too much math homework!" Bonnie started crying on Anne's shoulder, "I don't think she will like me very much! I stink at math! Math needs to start solving its own problems!!"

"Bonnie, don't worry. I will help you with your homework."

Bonnie looked up at Anne, "Really?"

"Really," Anne smiled weakly.

"Wow! Thanks, Anne!!" Bonnie wiped her nose on Anne's shirt.

Anne was disgusted and slowly pushed Bonnie off of her shoulder.

"Come on, or else we'll be late and end up in Madame Zoe's office *again*!"

Anne and Bonnie rushed inside the classroom where Mrs. Janet was writing equations on the blackboard. There were five rows of desks and all of the other kids were sitting with their hands crossed politely. All except for Jason who was at his desk slouching.

Mrs. Janet turned and snarled at Anne and Bonnie, "Have a seat you two troublemakers!"

Bonnie was holding back tears. Her face was turning red as she looked at all of the faces of the orphans staring at her.

Mrs. Janet snapped at Bonnie who still wasn't sitting down, "What's wrong with your face? Are you catching a cold standing there? My room isn't *that* cold."

"No, she just…gets red-faced sometimes," Anne said gritting her teeth.

"Well go on, sit down! Don't interfere with the lesson any further! You've already wasted five minutes of my time!"

Anne and Bonnie took their seats at the front of the classroom.

"Now listen you two, we have already started learning how to do pre-algebra—"

"But I didn't study!" Bonnie clasped her hands to her mouth and froze.

"I didn't we were going to have a *TEST!* Now, if we can stop having so many *interruptions,*" Mrs. Janet looked right at Bonnie who looked ashamed, "we can actually get some more knowledge into your little minds."

The board said: $8x+8=?$

"Now Anne or Bonnie, let's see how much you know already. What is the answer to this equation if x equals 2?" Mrs. Janet asked.

Anne and Bonnie had no answer. Everyone in the room was silent, no one really knew.

"Anyone else? Did we or did we not learn about pre-algebra for three weeks now?!"

Everyone stayed silent.

"Fine! If you all don't know, I guess we *will* have a test now after all!" Mrs. Janet opened a drawer in her desk and pulled out a stack of papers.

Anne looked in shock and said, "Um, Mrs. Janet?"

Mrs. Janet looked Anne's way and growled, "What?"

"Well, Bonnie and I haven't been able to do our preparation studies with all the cleaning that we had to do. We don't really know how to do pre-algebra."

"Well, maybe if you two shaped up and didn't get into trouble you would both pass this test with flying colors. So, it's your fault, not mine."

"When Mommy and Daddy come back here, they will help us. They'll put us in a real school," Bonnie mumbled as her eyes started to tear up.

"What did you say, Bonnie? Did you say…your Mommy and Daddy?" Mrs. Janet asked walking slowly to Bonnie's desk.

Jason was smiling. Anne froze. All of the other kids were murmuring to each other.

Bonnie looked frightened, wanting to reverse the past ten minutes.

"Let's make one thing clear; you're stuck here and with me and that is that! Here are your tests!" Mrs. Janet put the tests on their desks and walked back slowly, her heels making the only noise in the room.

Anne and Bonnie scowled but grabbed their pencils and started to do the test.

# ❧Chapter Nine❧

Later that day, Anne and Bonnie were sitting on a bench in the girls' locker room getting ready for P.E.

They were tying up their hair in ponytails and putting on some beat up running shoes. Their sweatshirts were dirty and their faded blue shorts were too tight for their waists.

"Anne, do we have to wear this?" Bonnie was trying to pull her sweatshirt down to cover the shorts.

"Does it look like we have anything else?" Anne pulled her shorts down some more and tried to brush the dirt off of her sweatshirt.

"I'd rather run naked than have to wear these shorts," Bonnie mumbled.

"That would *NOT* be a good idea," Anne said.

All of the orphans lined up in the chilly field. In front of the line was their P.E. teacher, Coach Curcio. She had blonde hair in a high ponytail and wore a yellow sweat suit with a whistle around her neck. She had big muscles and was obviously in good shape.

She blew her whistle and started walking toward the kids. They all made a path for her to walk down.

"Hello, class! Now I know it is cold, but that won't stop us from doing exercises. Besides, you will be less cold if you move around!" she boomed.

Bonnie was shivering. All of the other orphans were shaking too. The coach looked at Anne and Bonnie.

"Ah yes, the twin troublemakers. My name is Coach Curcio…welcome to my class. Now let's begin!"

They all started off with simple exercises like push-ups and jumping jacks. Anne and Bonnie started to warm up a little until a burst of wind crossed paths with the class and everyone started shivering again. Then it was time to run.

"When…are we…going…to be…done?" Bonnie asked running around a marked section of the meadow that served as a track. She was running so slowly she was almost walking. Everyone else was passing her with each lap.

"Come on, troublemaker! Use those legs!" Coach Curcio yelled.

Bonnie barely sped up and that only lasted a few seconds. Coach Curcio smacked herself on the forehead, "Come on! I know you can run faster!"

"I…haven't…done...P.E.…in…a while!" Bonnie gasped trying not to faint.

"Five more laps, everyone!"

"I…can't—"

Bonnie collapsed on the ground. Everyone almost trampled over her.

"Everyone, stop!" Coach Curcio blew her whistle.

"Bonnie!" Anne sat down and started to shake Bonnie. "Bonnie, wake up. Please!!"

Coach Curcio walked over and said, "I should get her inside, no one move. Anne you stay put, too. I'll take care of your sister." She lifted Bonnie off the ground, put her over her shoulder and went inside. After a few minutes, Jason came walking up to Anne.

"Wow, what a wimp," Jason laughed.

"Hey!" Anne barked, "If you think you can insult my sister in front of me…you're crazy!"

"Since you two look alike, I bet you're *both* wimps. Both retarded too!" A few kids, especially boys, started laughing.

"HEY!!!" Anne got right in Jason's face. "If you say one more thing about me or my sister, I'll…"

Jason smirked, "You'll what?"

Anne paused, then turned away.

"Yeah, nothing is what you'll do…that's what I thought!" Jason smirked.

Suddenly, Anne turned back around and punched him in the nose.

Everyone gasped.

Jason fell to the ground, his nose bleeding.

"Anne, what did you do?!" Maddie screamed.

Anne was shocked about what she did. "I'm sorry! I didn't mean to—,"

Jason started crying. Then he screeched for someone to help him.

Coach Curcio and Mrs. Janet heard the commotion and came running outside.

"Who did this?!" yelled the Coach.

Anne pleaded, "I didn't mean to! I didn't!"

"Young lady, come with me immediately!" yelled Mrs. Janet.

Anne was led inside to get in trouble *again* with Madame Zoe while Coach Curcio helped Jason try to stop the bleeding.

# Chapter Ten

"I can't believe it! You have broken two rules and you have been here for less than a month!" Madame Zoe said in her office. Bonnie was lying on a couch, recovering with a glass of water.

"I am so, so sorry. I didn't mean to punch him, I swear. He called me and my sister a wimp and retarded and I just…snapped."

"Well, there is no excuse for what you did. Even though I know Jason can be a handful. This is not the first time he's been involved with trouble." Her voice softened and she leaned down to Anne. "I know that you were just standing up for your sister, but I *have* to enforce the rules." She walked back to her desk. "You will be in detention for two weeks and will have extra homework. I am sorry, but attacking someone is definitely against the rules. You are dismissed."

Anne looked down at the floor and said, "I get it. Sorry again." She slowly got up and walked out of her office. Bonnie followed her out.

It was almost three o'clock. Anne was sitting on a bench outside of the playground doing her extra studies. The wind brushed her shoulders as she sighed with a deep breath. The sun hadn't shown for what seemed like almost a month now. She was surrounded by lifeless trees; the bark on the trees were as dead gray as the sky. At least spring was not far off.

The playground was filled with kids playing. Bonnie, who felt much better now, was on the swings. Jason was carefully shooting hoops with tissue in his nose and a black eye.

Anne looked up from her textbook and spotted Rose sitting near the swings looking her way. Rose's face was expressionless like it always was. Anne waved at her, but Rose didn't wave back. Anne soon figured out that Rose wasn't looking at her, she was looking behind her.

Anne turned around fast but saw nothing except the small forest behind her. She turned back around and Rose looked fearful. She had a look on her face that Anne had never seen her make before. Anne started to get worried. She walked over to Rose to ask her what was wrong. Louise quickly walked over to Rose too then sneered, "What are you doing, Anne? You're not supposed to be on the playground, remember?" She kneeled down to Rose, "What is wrong, Rose?" Rose had the same scared expression plastered on her face but said nothing.

Soon enough Ruby, Judy and a kid named Carson came over and looked worried.

"Why is she looking like that?" Carson asked.

Then a bunch of orphans walked over to Rose. Mrs. Janet came over, too.

"Rose, Rose Bellards! What is wrong, what is going on here?" Mrs. Janet asked. Rose said nothing again.

"She's been looking like this for about five minutes," Louise said, "right when *Anne* came over to her."

Everyone turned to Anne.

"Anne, what did you do?!" Mrs. Janet demanded.

"I didn't do anything, I swear! I thought Rose was staring at something behind me when I was sitting on the bench. I was just studying."

Rose still stared at the forest, then she took her bony finger and pointed toward the bench.

"Maybe a bird pooped on it," one of the boys laughed.

Mrs. Janet leaned into Rose's ear and quietly asked, "What is it that you see, Rose?"

"D— d—" Rose mumbled.

Everyone was waiting to hear what she had to say.

"What?" Mrs. Janet asked again.

Rose's eyes got very wide as she stuttered,

"D—Dad?"

Later that day back inside, the girls were trying to figure out what was going on. "She said 'Dad!'" Judy said walking around back and forth through the hall. The rest of the roommates (besides Rose who was downstairs) were sitting on the floor thinking about what Rose meant.

"Maybe she's just crazy," Ruby said.

"Or her dad used to sit on a bench and watch her when she was younger and that reminded her and she was just missing him," Caitlyn said.

"Well if you ask me," Louise said getting up, "she might be hallucinating."

"Or she's not right in the head," said Maddie.

"That is what I meant, crazy!!" Ruby snapped.

"Anne, what do you think?" Judy asked.

Everyone looked at Anne.

"I don't know, maybe she was just imagining that her dad was there. He died, right?"

Everyone nodded their heads.

Judy looked outside. The sun was setting fast.

"Dinner time soon. Come on everybody," she said.

Anne got up and Bonnie followed her out.

"Bonnie, what do you think about what Rose said?" asked Anne.

Bonnie paused, "I don't know, maybe she saw a ghost. I sure am hungry. Let's get downstairs!"

# ⊱Chapter Eleven⊱

The next day the girls were waking up and getting ready.

"Why are we having a meeting in the common room?" Bonnie asked as she pulled up her knee socks in the bathroom. Anne was on her bed putting on her sneakers. The rain outside poured down.

"I don't know, Bonnie."

"Do you know what it is about?"

"No."

"Why does it have to be so early?"

"Bonnie, stop asking me so many questions! I know as much as you do! Go ask Ruby or something." Anne finished tying her laces and started brushing her hair with an old brush. Bonnie strolled out of the bathroom and walked up to Ruby who was making her bed and was already dressed.

"Hey Bonnie," Ruby said putting her pillow on top of her neatly made bed.

"Hi, um, do you know why we're having a meeting?"

"No clue," Ruby said.

"Me neither," Maddie said as she walked up to Bonnie and Ruby.

"No one knows?" Bonnie started getting a little upset when Anne stormed in and asked in a flustered voice, "Who clogged up the toilet…again?"

Everyone pointed to Louise who's face turned bright red as she mumbled, "Sorry."

Anne, Bonnie, Ruby, Maddie, Rose, Louise, and Caitlyn lined up in the hallway with the rest of the girls. They met up with the boys in another hallway and then they all walked into the common room. Most people took passing glances at Rose who just looked straight forward sitting in her wheelchair.

Anne and Bonnie stared at the rows of old wooden chairs. When they sat down, they really started to notice the paintings and pictures on the walls all around them: ones with weird landscapes, ones with small children with their mothers, lots of photos of the orphanage. A rat scurried across the floor into a hole in the wall.

"Ew," some of the girls said cringing.

Madame Zoe walked out in front of everyone, no applause, just silence.

"Hello, everyone. Great day, isn't it?" she asked laughing a little, but everyone remained silent.

"Okay, good. It seems you are not in a silly mood and that's fine. What we are about to talk about is serious. Now I know there have been a lot of…" She looked around the room, "Well, as you all know accidents have been happening around here for the past few years ever since we opened. We might get in trouble if more occur, we might even get shut down. Now we know none of you kids would do serious harm to each other. Adults on the other hand, they can be a little crazy. We're not sure if anyone is entering our wonderful facility at night. So, we are locking the gates and all the doors from 9:00 at night to 6:00 in the morning. Make sure you are where you are supposed to be. We are not letting anyone in during those hours. We are just concerned for your safety. That is all, you are now dismissed."

Lots of kids started whispering, some of them started crying as they were terrified. Anne and Bonnie sat in silence.

"What a mess this all is," Anne said.

"At least we won't have to stay here forever," Bonnie said under her breath, "Mommy and Daddy will be back for us soon."

Anne turned to Bonnie after hearing what she had just said and felt as if she was about to cry. She ran out of the room and back upstairs. The crowd of kids were out of their seats walking out. Bonnie sat there by herself and started to cry.

"Please Mommy and Daddy, please come back to get us. Where are you?" Softly she began sobbing.

"Anne, it's okay, unlock the door," said Louise. She and Caitlyn were outside the bathroom door hearing Anne cry inside.

"It's hard, I know," Louise looked down, "I miss my parents, too."

"No! You don't understand! Bonnie still thinks that they are alive! But they are DEAD! They both died in a fire in our home, Bonnie and I were the only ones who were able to get out. They're gone…I was at the funeral."

"I know, Bonnie will soon realize it herself," Caitlyn said softly, "it's just her way of coping, I guess. It's okay, just come out and we can sort this thing through."

Anne cried and sniffed, "Just go away."

Louise and Caitlyn sighed and walked out of the room.

The day passed on into the afternoon, then passed on into the evening. Anne was silent to her sister; she didn't know how to handle Bonnie's belief their parents were still alive and coming back for them. She went to bed that night sad and confused.

That was Friday. Saturday morning dawned and Bonnie woke up in a great mood.

"No school!" Bonnie shouted as the rest of the girls were getting up.

"Yeah…" Anne sighed as she rose from her bed.

"What's wrong, Anne? You haven't been talking lately. Does it have something to do with the meeting and possible night time intruders? I don't believe that's happening."

"I don't think that's happening either. I'm trying to solve this mystery, but it's a tough one. I think it's someone here at Firefly Meadows but I can't be sure right now."

"My friend Amanda told me it was a bad spirit in this place causing all the problems, but she couldn't tell me who the spirit was."

"Who are you talking about, Bonnie?!"

"The girl who lives in the basement. I can prove it to you if you want. Do you want to go down in the basement with me?

Anne closed her eyes tiredly. "Bonnie," she yawned, "we aren't allowed to go to the basement. Besides, the last thing I want to do is get in trouble again." Anne opened her eyes and turned to Bonnie…who wasn't there.

"Bonnie?" Anne shot out of bed, sprinted down the stairs and ran up to the basement door. Bonnie was standing in front of it.

"Bonnie! Let's go back upstairs! If we get caught again, we will get in trouble for a year!"

"Anne, do your trick, unlock this door. I promise it will help with figuring out this mystery!" Anne looked around…*she couldn't resist* a good mystery. How much more trouble could she get in? What would Nancy Drew do? Slowly she picked the lock with her hairpin and opened the door.

They could see the first three steps of the stairs, but the light ended there. Anne gulped.

"Come on, Anne!" Bonnie began down the stairs.

Anne slowly stepped onto the first basement step, scared that she was making yet another mistake at Firefly Meadows.

"Go to the next step, Anne, keep going," Anne told herself.

She took the next step down, sinking more and more into the darkness. Anne took the last step she could see and was afraid of taking another.

"Bonnie?! Where are you! Stop fooling around!"

"Anne?" A voice blurted from down below. "Come here!"

A light suddenly came on. Anne looked down noticing that she had to take five more steps before she was on the ground. There was no other way out, no door leading outside, just a stack of wooden boxes against the back wall. Right next to the boxes was Bonnie and right next to her was a file cabinet.

"Bonnie…" a voice whispered.

"Amanda?" Bonnie said, "Anne, I hear her. She's here somewhere!"

"I don't hear anyone," said Anne.

All of a sudden, Amanda appeared to Bonnie.

"I need to show you something, Bonnie," said Amanda, "something that will answer many of your questions."

Bonnie looked around and everything started spinning. Almost like a movie, Bonnie started seeing scenes about the orphanage.

"Bonnie, are you OK?" asked Anne as she watched Bonnie close her eyes. Bonnie did not answer, she just stood there watching the visions Amanda was placing in her mind.

At first, she saw the Dining Hall, except it looked like the Dining Hall that she saw when she met up with Amanda last time, empty and dirty. There were wheelchairs scattered around, old plates still out on the tables. It all looked abandoned.

*"The door,"* whispered Amanda's voice.

The scene went upstairs to the scary room that Anne and Bonnie were trapped in a month ago. It showed a man inside, crying and screaming and clawing at the walls, ripping the wallpaper.

The man had a black beard and piercing brown eyes. His hair was dirty and messy and he had chains on his ankles that were attached to his bed. On the end of his bed was a file holder that read, *"Grant Bellards."*

The next clip zoomed out of the room and showed attendants running to him. They took off his chains and dragged him out of the room down the hall and to the stairs.

Bonnie looked around, scared.

The vision zoomed out again, down the stairs and to the basement door.

*"The basement..."* whispered Amanda's voice again as the scene zoomed down into the basement, except it looked different from what

Anne and Bonnie were just seeing moments ago. Now lights were on and there was a large door where the stack of wooden boxes are now. The file cabinet was still there…

Amanda's voice whispered,

*"Look in the file cabinet, you will find him…"*

Bonnie was breathing fast. Never in her life has she been scared like this. The attendants were now in the basement forcing the bearded man to the large door. As one of them unlocked it, the scene revealed a hallway with several doors on either side. They continued to drag the bearded man down the hall then into one of the rooms. It looked like a hospital room. The man was then strapped down to a table where another man with a surgical mask filled up a needle with some kind of drug.

"Hold him still," the man said as he injected the drug into his arm. The bearded man screamed for them to stop what they were doing…but they didn't.

*"The roof…"* Amanda's voice whispered.

The scene shot up to the roof of the building where a storm was raging. Bonnie could now see Amanda on the roof and realized that this must be when Firefly Meadows was an orphanage. As lightning flashed, Amanda was backing closer and closer to the edge. A hooded figure was closing in on her as she yelled,

"No...no...NO!"

The hooded figure gave Amanda a strong push sending her screaming over the edge and down to the wet pavement below.

*"I didn't jump..."*

*"I was pushed..."*

*"It was Bellards..."*

# ∞ Chapter Twelve ∞

"STOP GETTING INSIDE MY HEAD!!!" Bonnie yelled. She dropped and started rolling on the floor screaming and crying and smacking herself in the head. She was back in the basement with only Anne.

"Bonnie? Bonnie! Stop doing that to yourself!!" Anne said in a very concerned voice.

"Where did they go?!" Bonnie asked looking around.

"Bonnie what just happened?! What did you see?" asked Anne.

"It was Amanda! Didn't you see her?

"No Bonnie, I didn't see anyone. You just kind of fell into a trance."

"She is able to talk to me. I can see her sometimes and she gets in my head to show me…things. Weird things. And it just happened again!"

"OK, Bonnie, I believe you," said Anne in a comforting way, "what did…Amanda tell you?"

"Grant Bellards did it…" Bonnie mumbled.

"What, Bonnie?"

"*Grant Bellards did it!* He killed Amanda and is probably causing all of the bad things that happen around here!" Bonnie stood up and continued, "I saw a vision of him getting dragged through a door that is here behind these boxes. There are, like, old hospital rooms back in there. He must have been a patient here when this building was an insane asylum years ago."

Anne froze. "This place was a what?"

"An insane asylum," Bonnie repeated.

"Bonnie, do you know what that means?"

Bonnie nodded her head up and down then said, "No. What does it mean?"

Anne sighed then said, "Well, it is where crazy people are sent, it's like a prison for insane people…people can run tests on the patients there and try to cure what makes them crazy. All sorts of things happen at those places…how do you know this place used to be an asylum?"

"Amanda showed me the last time I was down here." Bonnie then looked down feeling ashamed. "I know we aren't allowed down here, but look here." Bonnie turned around and opened the old file cabinet that was still there in the basement. She searched through the first drawer looking at lots of files. "She said his file is in here, we can find out more about him."

Anne looked at the staircase, hoping that no one was coming to the Dining Hall. She was suddenly excited. This *was* becoming a real mystery.

"Anne, this last drawer is locked. Help me!" She shined the flashlight right on the lock.

Anne pulled out her hair pin and carefully unlocked the bottom drawer.

Bonnie pulled open the drawer and started to flip through the files that were in there until they reached one that read "Grant Bellards."

Bonnie handed Anne the file. "This is the one."

"Why is this so important?" Anne asked.

"Because Amanda said it was. Just read it," Bonnie said.

Anne opened up the file. She saw a picture of a man with a black beard and brown eyes, he had a look of horror on his face. Attached to the picture were several pieces of paper.

"Read it!" Bonnie demanded.

Anne sighed and started reading out loud, "Grant Bellards, the longest stay here at Firefly Meadows Asylum—" Anne choked the words out, "he escaped five times in total." Anne took a deep breath and continued, "He is dangerous, one of the most violent patients ever. He stays in the last room in the hallway. He claws the wallpaper, finds ways to get pieces of paper and writes to his 'imaginary people.' Grant claimed he had a wife and a newborn daughter in a nearby town, but there is no evidence of them existing. He ended up dying from his experimental treatments in September of 1950."

Anne let out a sigh, "Bonnie, these are just old files from back when this place was an asylum."

"But Anne, that's the thing," Bonnie snatched the file and reread the words, "he claimed he had a wife and a newborn daughter in a nearby town, that has to mean something!"

Anne snatched the file back, "Bonnie, these are just files about people that were crazy and are dead now."

"But why would Amanda bring him up like he was the one that pushed her off this building?"

"Bonnie, that's impossible. If I know my facts, Firefly Meadows Orphanage was opened in 1952. It says here that Grant Bellards died in 1950. Don't you see, Bonnie? It couldn't be him. You can believe in ghosts all you want but I don't! Now let's get out of here, please!"

Anne and Bonnie quietly went up the stairs with the file that they found, entered the Dining Hall without anyone seeing them and carefully closed the door behind them. Then they went upstairs to the girls' wing.

Anne opened the door to their room and tiredly walked inside. Bonnie followed.

"Anne," Bonnie said.

"What?"

"You should put that file under your bed so no one will suspect us."

"Good idea."

"I'm going to get a snack, see ya later!" Bonnie left the room in search of food. Anne looked around the room noticing the badly drawn pictures made in art class by Bonnie taped to the window. She laughed a little at the picture she made of a pig eating bacon.

"Oh Bonnie, that's cannibalism!" Anne chuckled.

Then she noticed a notepad on top of the dresser. She didn't want to be a total snoop, but she couldn't help herself. As Anne picked it up, she noticed it was a suspect list.

She was pleasantly surprised to find that someone besides herself was looking for the culprit.

The list read:

*suspects*
*Reagan*
*Judy*
*Madame Zoe*
*Mr. Claude*
*Jason*

"Huh, someone else is also trying to solve the mystery," Anne whispered.

Then she noticed the last words written on the paper, and she couldn't believe what she read:

*main suspect*
*Bonnie*

# ೞChapter Thirteenೞ

Anne was startled knowing that someone suspected her own sister of hurting the orphans.

"She doesn't even know how to run fast without tripping. Besides, orphans have been getting hurt way before Bonnie and I arrived," Anne muttered to herself.

She tore the piece of paper with suspects off of the pad and stuffed it in her pocket.

It was Sunday night. Anne, Bonnie, Louise, and Rose sat next to each other outside looking at the orphanage. The lights coming from inside gleamed through the windows. They could see kids inside eating, laughing, or doing secret handshakes in the Dining Hall. Rose was sitting in her chair a few feet away from the girls just staring off into the lifeless, dark, grey sky.

"Who do *you* suspect might be the Firefly Meadows culprit?" Anne asked Louise who was excited that in less than a day she wouldn't have to look after Rose anymore.

"If you ask me…"

"And I did," Anne laughed.

"Well, I would say Reagan," she whispered. Louise watched Reagan in the window— she was brushing her curly hair inside the Dining Hall, smiling at the boys while flipping her hair side to side as she brushed.

"How do you figure? She looks completely harmless," Anne said. They watched as Reagan made a funny face at Jason as he walked past her table.

"Well, only I know this but I guess I can tell you because I trust you," Louise leaned in next to Anne's ear, "I have seen Reagan wake up in the middle of the night and leave the girls' wing. I feel like she is meeting someone to do something…but I don't know what."

"Anne, I want to go back inside," said Bonnie in a weak voice, "I'm tired and I just want to go back in."

"OK, fine," said Anne, "we'll see you later, Louise."

"Bye, guys. Gotta take care of you-know-who," said Louise.

Bonnie hustled back towards the orphanage. Anne quickly caught up with her.

"Are you feeling all right, Bonnie? What's wrong with you?" asked Anne.

"Something just doesn't feel right, something…oh you wouldn't understand!"

Anne huffed at Bonnie when she turned and noticed Louise running towards them very fast.

"Rose—she's…she's gone!" Louise said breathing hard.

"What?!" gasped Anne.

"One minute she was there, but now she's gone. Her chair and everything!"

"Okay—this is serious…quick, let's go back to where she was."

Anne, Bonnie and Louise ran back to where they were sitting. Then it began to rain. Anne looked outside the open gates and saw Rose way off in the distance.

"Over there! She's way down the road! Rose, come back!!" Anne yelled.

Louise and Bonnie ran over to Anne. They saw the small image of Rose in her wheelchair surrounded by the meadows. The tall grass was being tackled by the wind. Dark clouds filled the entire sky. The rain started increasing.

"How did she get that far that fast?!" Louise screamed.

"Come on!" Anne yelled over the storm.

The three girls ran out of the gates. They could only see a few inches in front of them because of the rain and how dark it had become. They definitely couldn't see Rose anymore.

"I can't see anything! ROSE!!!" Anne yelled. No answer, just rain. "Where did you go?!"

She looked back at the orphanage. All the lights were still on. It was only a little after five o' clock but already dark outside because of the storm.

"Hello?!" Anne started to freak out. She couldn't see Bonnie *or* Louise now. She could see the forest. It looked a lot creepier when it was dark. She shivered and tried to figure out how to get out of this mess. Out of the dark she heard a voice that sounded a lot like Bonnie's.

"Anne! Help me!"

"Where are you?!" Anne ran around the meadow searching helplessly for Bonnie and Louise.

"I'm over here, I can't see you or anyone!" Bonnie yelled from the far side of the pouring rain.

"But where?!" Anne kept on running towards Bonnie's voice.

She eventually found Bonnie. She was sitting, holding onto her knees on the muddy ground at the top of a small hill that led down to a lake.

"Bonnie! Stand up!" Anne yelled.

Bonnie got up. Her grey sweatpants stained with mud, then she slipped and fell on the ground again.

"Bonnie! Get back up!" Anne held her hand out for Bonnie to grab. The mud on her hands quickly smeared all over Anne's hand and arm. Bonnie got back up and wiped her hands all over Anne's yellow shirt. Anne groaned as she watched the rain and the mud make her shirt look like a dark, ugly mess.

"Bonnie, have you seen Louise or Rose?"

"No, have you?"

"No!" Anne yelled.

Anne and Bonnie carefully made their way toward the center of the meadow. As they walked, they held out their hands like they might run into something.

Then they heard Louise screaming from the not too distant woods.

"Louise! It sounded like her voice came from the woods. Let's go Bonnie!"

"No!" Bonnie yelled, "I am *not* going into those woods."

"Bonnie, we have to find Louise and Rose and get back to the orphanage before the curfew. Do you want to get in trouble with Madame Zoe again?!" Anne crossed her arms and almost lost her balance because of the wind. Bonnie didn't respond.

"Fine then!" Anne got behind Bonnie and shoved her towards the woods, but she slipped and fell into the mud. Bonnie toppled over too and became even more muddy than before. She quickly got back up and wiped her hands on Anne's face.

"Hey!" Anne wiped off the mud and snarled at Bonnie, "What was that for?!"

"What do you think? You pushed me in the mud!" Bonnie shoved Anne again.

"Well I'm just trying to get through this. You're not being any help. In fact, you've been embarrassing me ever since we got here. Ever since you were born!!"

"Hey! Watch it, Anne! YOU'RE the one who's always complaining and angry. Why do you get so mad and frustrated all the time?!" Bonnie demanded.

"YOU DON'T UNDERSTAND WHAT IS HAPPENING?!" Anne screamed, "WE LOST ROSE AND WE'RE AT THE EDGE OF A FOREST IN THE RAIN. WE HAVE TO GET BACK TO THE ORPHANAGE VERY SOON OR WE ARE GOING TO CATCH A COLD FROM BEING IN THIS WEATHER *AND* WE WILL BE SUSPECTED OF MURDER IF WE DON'T FIND ROSE!!"

Bonnie replied, "Actually we'll be suspected of two murders if we don't find Louise either."

Anne boiled with anger. She shoved Bonnie and sent her toppling over. The girls kept fighting with each other until they heard Louise yell from the woods again, "I found her! I found Rose! Come quickly!!"

# ❧Chapter Fourteen❧

The twins stopped fighting and got up. Anne wiped as much mud off of her face as possible and shouted, "Louise needs us! We have to go help her!"

Bonnie hesitated but then said, "You're right, OK."

Anne grabbed Bonnie's hand and they both started into the woods.

"Louise?!" Anne screamed. She and Bonnie struggled through the mud and leaves in the forest. Trees surrounded them like watchful guards, clinging to their every move and every word.

"Anne! I don't like this!" Bonnie said. The winds that passed through the trees sounded like whistling in the air— as if someone was near her.

"Louise! Rose! I know you can hear me! We're coming!" Anne yelled.

The rain stopped all of a sudden. The wind died down. The trees stopped watching them. Everything was calm and silent for the first time since they left Firefly Meadows. Then a voice came out of the woods.

"Over here…" It was Louise. She was using all of her strength to push a soaking wet Rose out of the woods.

"What happened? How did she get all the way out here?" Anne asked, "Rose, how did you get this far out by yourself?"

Rose slowly looked up at Anne and Bonnie then back at Louise before saying in a hushed voice, "I wasn't by myself…"

The girls stood with their jaws open. Then Anne asked while nervously looking around, "Rose, was someone pushing you out here?"

Rose nodded yes.

"Let's just get out of here, now!" All three girls helped push Rose out of the woods, back onto the road and back through the gates of Firefly Meadows.

When they got there, Bonnie was trudging behind Louise. Anne was in the front leading the way.

"I'm hungry," Louise complained.

"Aren't we all," Anne mumbled, "We've got to
get back inside before a staff member see us caked

in mud...we'll get in trouble for sure!" Just then they heard a voice yell, "Stop it, Jason!"

Louise turned around instantly. "That sounded like Reagan."

Jason and Reagan were out on the playground in the dark. Who knows WHAT they were doing, but they were not rain soaked so they must have come outside after the storm blew over.

"Reagan, it's Anne and Bonnie and Louise and Rose. We need your help!" Anne said in a loud whisper.

Jason and Reagan walked over, confused as to what was going on. Then Reagan saw what they looked like in the light of the windows and gasped, "What happened to you?

You look like you took a mud bath! Quick, come with me!"

The girls cautiously went inside the Dining Hall area. Judy was still eating when she saw the group of mud-soaked girls with Reagan and Jason.

"Woah, what happened to you guys?" Judy asked.

"Judy, we need to get Rose and her wheelchair cleaned up. Help me get her into the bathroom over there."

"The coast is clear," said Jason not looking directly at Anne, "you girls get upstairs and change before Madame Zoe sees you!"

Louise, Anne and Bonnie all hurried up the stairs hoping not even Mr. Claude would see them.

Caitlyn and Sydney came racing over to Anne, Bonnie and Louise. As soon as they saw what condition they were in, they were stunned.

"What happened to you?!" Sydney said nudging Louise playfully, "Did you do some mud wrestling?"

"No, we were—" Anne's voice trailed off.

"In the meadows," Louise cut in. "We were looking for—" Louise's voice trailed off, too.

"We were looking for my—" Bonnie's face went blank, "pig. I didn't tell you but I made friends with a wild pig the other day and he ran off last night. So…we were looking for my pig…we didn't find it."

Caitlyn and Sydney stood there silent. Anne, Bonnie, and Louise's faces went pale.

"Oh…" Sydney said making a strange expression, "that makes… sense."

"Are you kidding us?" Caitlyn asked crossing her arms.

"If you really are telling the truth, what is the pig's name?" Sydney asked.

"Um—Oh, its name was…" Bonnie looked around and opened her mouth, but nothing came out. Anne hit Bonnie on the back like she was helping her burp, but what came out of her was the name, "Frank."

There was a long silence.

"Okay then," Caitlyn said in a tone that let them know that she thought they were crazy, "Bye!"

She and Sydney turned and went back into their room.

"They bought it!" Bonnie laughed.

"They almost did," Anne mumbled.

"Well, we better pretend this didn't happen and get cleaned up before Madame Zo—"

Louise stopped talking and stared up at the woman who was standing in front of them crossed-armed. It was Madame Zoe, and she did not look happy at all.

"Louise…Anne…Bonnie…" Madame Zoe glared.

"Yes?" the girls sighed.

"I want you in my office first thing tomorrow morning, we are going to have a lot to talk about! Right now, get cleaned up and go to bed!!"

# ❧Chapter Fifteen❧

Louise, Anne and Bonnie sat in Madame Zoe's office the next morning waiting for their punishment.

Anne sat in a chair secretly crying, not sure what Madame Zoe was going to do now. She looked out the window at the kids playing on the playground. By the bench next to the swings she saw Rose. She and her chair were all cleaned up and she was busy drawing on a pad of paper. Ruby was the assistant to Rose today so she was close by.

"Anne, you said that the three of you thought Rose just rolled herself off into the woods and the three of you went to find her?" asked Madame Zoe.

"I know," she sighed staring at the floor. "She was here the whole time. It was a wild goose chase. We should have come to you or Mrs. Janet first. I'm really sorry."

Madame Zoe sat down at her desk and kept glaring at the three girls who just hung their heads knowing that they were in deep trouble.

"Well," Madame Zoe said almost gritting her teeth, "you left the grounds of Firefly Meadows without permission, and in a storm. You could have been hurt or possibly killed! You know how things are around here and how I have to make sure that nothing happens to anymore of you children! I am very disappointed in each and every one of you. I am especially disappointed in *you*, Anne."

Anne sighed.

"Anne and Bonnie Bleaster, you two have only been here for a little over a month now and you have already gotten into trouble *twice*," Madame Zoe said then looked directly at Anne, "three times for one of you. So…I am giving you all detention for two weeks! Anne, you already have two weeks of detention so that means four weeks total for you!"

Louise and Anne sighed. Bonnie's eyes started to tear up.

"Madame Zoe, where *is* detention?" Bonnie asked.

"Mrs. Janet's classroom. Now leave my office. When schooling is over, I will let Mrs. Janet know you three will be there after class is over."

Madame Zoe got up and opened the door for the girls. When they walked out, the door slammed behind them.

"Well, shoot," Louise sighed, "I am so sorry for this. You both don't deserve this. I was responsible for Rose and you were just trying to help."

"It's OK. Anyway, we have to be at Mrs. Janet's classroom in thirty minutes," Anne said.

Bonnie watched from downstairs as the kids walked to class, some were holding onto books or homework assignments while others were sitting in the lounge doing their school work.

"Well, what do we do now, Anne?" Bonnie sat on a bench next to the staircase.

"I guess we just …wait."

Anne sat next to Bonnie who started biting her nails. Anne then reached into her pocket and pulled out the list of suspects she got from the notepad. She looked at it and wondered who wrote out the list and why Bonnie was on it. *Bonnie doesn't even know how to run fast without tripping. There's no way she could sneak around and pull off a mystery!* Anne thought.

"Anne?" Bonnie turned to her.

"Yeah?"

"Do you still have that file on Grant Bellards under your bed?"

"Yes, but Bonnie, we shouldn't look at it right now," Anne closed her eyes, rubbing her forehead from a headache. "In fact, we shouldn't even *have* the file. After detention, I'm going to turn it into Ms. Maria and say that we found it while we were cleaning or something."

Anne opened her eyes and realized that Bonnie wasn't sitting next to her anymore. She had run off! Anne jumped off the bench and started running down the hallway. No sign of Bonnie.

She went into their room and saw that the bathroom door was shut. Anne went to open it but it was locked.

"Bonnie, are you in there?" Anne whispered.

She tried opening it again.

"Bonnie?" Anne waited for her to respond through the door. "Open the door if you're in there…you know I can just pick the lock."

The door slowly clicked and Anne opened it. Bonnie was sitting on the floor holding a piece of paper.

"Bonnie?! What got into you, why did you run off? We can't be late for class! Bonnie, what are you holding?" Anne took the piece of paper. Bonnie's hand didn't move and looked like it was holding onto an invisible piece of paper.

"I remember seeing this list of names before and it just hit me, I had to run back here and make sure," said Bonnie.

"Bonnie, this is the list of all the girls here that was on the wall…you've seen this before. It just shows the names of who is assigned to this room." Then Anne looked down and there was one name circled in red, the same color red as the crayon that Bonnie was holding in her other hand. It was Rose's full name.

"Rose Marie Bellards. *Bellards.*"

Anne realized what it meant: *Rose could be the daughter of Grant Bellards!*

Bonnie was still frozen in her position on the floor.

"Bonnie? Bonnie, snap out of it!" Anne splashed water over Bonnie's face from the sink.

Bonnie shook her head and looked around, "Anne? Anne! Where is the list of names?"

"Calm down, it's right here." Anne held it in front of Bonnie who stood up. They both looked at it in wonder.

"What do we do about it?" Anne asked.

"What do we do about what?"

"Bonnie, you were the one who circled Rose's name. You were the one who figured it out."

"Did I circle it."

"Yes, Bonnie! The red crayon is in your hand!"

"It is?" Bonnie looked down at her hand then made a laugh that sounded like she just hiccupped and laughed at the same time. "Oh yeah, I guess I did circle it. I thought I would have chosen green though."

Anne sighed. "Fine, you forgot that you circled it, but it means that Rose might be the daughter of Grant Bellards. Remember that letter we found in his room?"

Bonnie nodded her head.

"Well, if it's true, then that letter was talking *directly* to Rose. We should go get it for her after detention." Anne's heart then skipped a beat as she realized that they were late for class. "Bonnie, we have to *go*!"

Anne grabbed Bonnie's hand and they ran down the hallway and down the stairs to Mrs. Janet's classroom. When they got there, they saw three desks placed at the very front of the room. Louise was in one of them sitting quietly with her hands folded. Right in front of those desks was Mrs. Janet's desk. Mrs. Janet was sitting there glaring at Anne and Bonnie.

"You two are late," she growled, "Sit down!"

Anne and Bonnie hung their heads down and walked over to the desks. Class was now in session.

After class was over and all the other kids left, Mrs. Janet addressed Anne, Bonnie and Louise.

"You three did a pretty bad thing going out of the gates at night in the middle of the storm. Going into the meadows *then* into the forest. You should all be ashamed."

"But Mrs. Janet! We were looking for Rose! We thought that…"

"I don't care what you thought, you did it anyway! You can't make an excuse to me about *any* of it. Now you three will be sitting in here for two hours, each day, for *two* weeks. No books, no drawing, no anything. Just sitting!"

Anne, Louise, and Bonnie had their heads down.

Mrs. Janet headed towards the door to leave the classroom but stopped herself, turned around and added, "I will be back in two hours, and if someone moves from their seat…" She turned around and showed a sheet of white paper, then ripped it all the way down the middle and laughed as she walked out.

When she left the room, Anne, Bonnie and Louise sighed.

A few minutes went by when Anne turned to Louise and said,

"Hey, Louise."

"Yeah?"

Anne pulled out the piece of notebook paper with the names of suspects that she found, trying to keep Bonnie from seeing it.

"Did you write this?" Anne handed the paper to Louise who looked at it in wonder.

"No, I didn't. You should ask Maddie. She has been working on the mystery, too." Louise handed the paper of suspects back to Anne who sighed, "This is going to be a long two hours."

"OK, time is up. *Good work*, girls," Mrs. Janet said sarcastically as she came back into the classroom. "I'll see you all next week for school—and detention." Mrs. Janet closed the blinds to the windows in the classroom. Bonnie was barely awake and Anne was drooping in her chair while Louise was sitting up straight, excited that they would finally be getting out detention.

"You are all—" Louise ran out of the classroom while Anne and Bonnie slowly got out of their seats. "dismissed…" Mrs. Janet shook her head and turned around to wipe down the blackboard.

Anne and Bonnie walked out of the room, Bonnie in front and Anne walking slowly behind her.

"Oh, and Anne," Mrs. Janet said.

Anne stopped and turned around. Bonnie waited by the doorway.

"Your detention is for four weeks, correct?" Mrs. Janet had her arms crossed.

"Oh, um, yes. I think so."

"Well, maybe you could help me clean the classroom…since you're going to spending extra time here anyway," Mrs. Janet said with a smirk.

"Oh, okay," Anne said in a defeated voice as she walked out.

A rumble of thunder came from outside. "Great, another storm," Anne said.

She went downstairs into the Dining Hall where she got in line with her sister and Louise. Lots of orphans were there already eating and talking.

"Hey, Anne, I got to go to the bathroom," said Bonnie.

"Okay."

"Grab me a tray please, you know what I like!" Bonnie got out of line and ran up the stairs until she almost tripped...so then she started walking. Another rumble of thunder crashed through the darkening skies outside.

A few kids walked past her down the hallway toward the Dining Hall as Bonnie headed back to her room. She stopped and noticed that the lights were getting dim further on down the hall. Something compelled her to keep walking. She passed room after room until she stopped at Grant Bellards' door.

"I should go get Anne to open this door again," Bonnie mumbled, "Rose deserves to have that note from her father."

Slowly, the door opened by itself.

# ∾Chapter Sixteen∾

Lightning flashed through the Dining Hall windows. Anne looked at the staircase outside of the Dining Hall, no sign of Bonnie. She looked down at her tray of food and it looked like slop. Next to her tray was another tray of slop she got for Bonnie, which was now getting cold.

"Come on, Bonnie," Anne whispered to herself, "I even got you *two* stale breads!"

Anne got up and walked up the staircase near the girls' wing to try to find out where Bonnie went. Thunder roared again and the lights flickered a little.

She peeked into the girls' room. No sign of her. Not even in the bathroom. "Bonnie?" she called out.

Soon she heard a shriek from down the hall that sounded like her sister. "Bonnie I'm coming!" Anne yelled.

Anne ran down to the end of the hall and saw that the last room on the left was open. As she entered the room, she couldn't believe what she saw. Bonnie was cowering and screaming in the corner and a hooded figure was closing in on her!

"Bonnie, get out of there!" pleaded Anne.

"I can't! This person is so strong, I can't get around!"

Lightning flashed outside the windows followed immediately by thunder. The storm was upon Firefly Meadows. Soon, other girls began running down the hall toward all the noise; Ruby, Caitlyn, Reagan, Sydney, Louise and Judy, among others.

"What's going on here, Anne?!" asked Ruby as the other girls caught up. They screamed when they saw the hooded figure.

"I knew that it was true!" shouted Reagan.

"Help me!!" pleaded Bonnie.

"Help my sister!" yelled Anne.

Judy and Louise looked at each other and nodded. They ran into the room and

grabbed the figure by each arm. The figure tossed them around but they held on.

"We need help!" screamed Louise.

Anne and some of the other girls burst in and tackled the hooded person to the ground. Bonnie ran over to the doorway with the other girls. The figure was so strong that even though there were several girls hanging on, the person was able to stand back up. Anne ran around to the still-hidden face of the person and grabbed the hood of the raincoat.

"Who are you?!" yelled Anne as she threw back the hood revealing the person's face. It was…

Rose.

Lightning and thunder crashed at the same time as everyone screamed in disbelief.

"It can't be!" yelled Caitlyn.

"How is she able to do this?!" shouted Sydney.

"Rose! What is happening?! Why? How?" asked Anne, dumbstruck.

Rose said nothing. Her eyes were glazed over and white. Suddenly her body started to loosen in the grip of all the girls holding her. She began to slump down to the floor.

Bonnie's eyes got very wide as she gasped and yelled to her sister, "Anne, it's him!"

"What are you talking about?!" asked Anne.

What no one but Bonnie could see was *the spirit of Grant Bellards rising from Rose's collapsed body*. There was no mistaking his beard and piercing eyes. He stared at Bonnie and began to float right towards her. The lights again began to flicker.

"It's Grant Bellards! He was controlling Rose and now he's coming right at me!"

The spirit kept moving towards Bonnie with an evil stare.

"Run, Bonnie!" yelled Anne.

As soon as Bonnie raced out of the doorway she ran into Madame Zoe and Ms. Maria as they were rushing down the hallway to find the rest of the girls.

"Girls, what is everyone doing in this room! No matter. Everyone to the basement right now! We think that a tornado is part of this storm and it's right on us!"

Bonnie looked back in fear but Grant Bellards was no longer there. He had vanished.

"Everyone, help each other! Don't gather any belongings just get downstairs now!" shouted Ms. Maria. Then she spotted Rose on the floor with the other girls. "What is Rose doing up here?! Someone, carry her! We have to go now!!"

The girls were still confused and looked to Anne for direction.

"It's okay, I'll explain later," said Anne, "Rose is all right but I don't think she can walk now. Pick her up and let's go!" Louise and a few others scooped up Rose's now weak body and began to carry her out.

Everyone shuffled down the stairs as a loud noise began to rise up from outside. It sounded like a giant train. As everyone ran through the Dining Hall and to the basement door that Mr. Claude had just unlocked, Madame Zoe was pointing a flashlight and frantically waving all the boys and girls down the stairs.

"It's going to be fine, hurry please! Watch your step and watch out for each other!"

The younger children were crying as the older kids were helping them get settled in the basement.

"Come on, everyone, you know the drill! We all have to be down there where it's safe!" Madame Zoe was still in the Dining Hall waving the last few kids and staff to go down the stairs. Then she started down the steps. Mr. Claude shut the door and locked it from inside the basement.

The noise of the tornado made everyone huddle in fear as they watched Mr. Claude creak down the last step. It was very crowded in the basement.

"Will we die?" asked a frightened young girl.

"No, dear. We are all safe," Ms. Maria said, even though she sounded unsure.

Bonnie squeezed her way through all of the kids to the other side of the room next to Anne who was by the wooden boxes.

"Anne?"

"Yes?"

"I'm scared."

"I am too, Bonnie."

The train sound got louder and louder until they felt the ground shaking. Screaming began as the children feared for their lives. The sounds of stones and walls collapsing filled the air. Tables and chairs were hitting up against the basement door and glass was shattering everywhere.

Bonnie started sobbing.

"I love you, Anne," she cried.

"I love you, too, Bonnie."

Anne started crying, too.

They held each other and waited for the doom that must be coming.

The sound of a bird chirping outside of the basement door made Anne wake up and look around. She was still in the basement...and still alive. Everyone around looked to be asleep.

"What happened?" Anne could barely see because it was so dark, but some light was shining through the door at the top of the stairs.

*Is it morning?* she thought.

She looked at the orphans lying on the dirt floor.

Madame Zoe, Mrs. Janet and Ms. Maria were lying near the stairs along with Mr. Claude who was slumped over next to them.

Anne looked around for Bonnie who was no longer next to her. She looked around the basement and noticed someone standing in front of the side wall. It was Bonnie!

Bonnie looked as if she was crying and talking with someone.

"Bonnie?" Anne walked over to her, cautious of the kids lying on the floor.

"She can't see you," Bonnie said to the wall.

Anne looked confused.

Bonnie looked at the wall as if it was telling her something. Bonnie nodded, still teary eyed, looked at Anne and grabbed her arm.

"Bonnie?! What are you doing—" Anne stopped talking when she saw what was now in front of her, something that was not there just a second before Bonnie grabbed her: It was an open doorway glowing with a bright light.

In that doorway stood Mr. and Mrs. Bleaster...Anne and Bonnie's parents.

They had a yellow glow outlining their bodies. They looked at Anne and smiled.

"Mom? Dad?" Anne's eyes started to tear up.

"Yes, it's us," their Mom said softly.

"I tried to tell you, Anne," Bonnie still had her arm latched to Anne's, "I told you they would come back."

Anne smiled but was confused.

"I don't understand what's going on," Anne said.

"I think you do. Your sister has always had a gift to see things that others cannot. By physically connecting with her you can share her sight. That's why you can see us now," their Dad said softly.

"What about everyone here?" asked Anne, "Why is everyone still lying on the ground? Are they dead?"

"No dear, they are asleep. The spirit world is doing some things right now. They will be awake soon."

Then Anne had a thought.

"Since you really can see ghosts, Bonnie, that means you really saw Grant Bellards. He could still be here!"

"No. He was, but not anymore," their Mom said.

Then the basement door opened at the top of the staircase by itself. Anne and Bonnie gazed up there and saw blue sky outside of the door.

"Umm…where is the Dining Hall?" Bonnie asked.

"The tornado blew it down," their Dad said.

"Most of the building has been destroyed," their Mom said with a smile.

"But that's bad!" Anne said, "Now we have nowhere to live!"

"No, it is a good thing," their Mom said, "That means that the spirits that were trapped here are now free."

"What?" Anne asked.

"You know by now that this place was an asylum," Mr. Bleaster said, "So many patients died here because of what the cruel people who ran this place did to them. They treated them like animals to do research on and experiment with. Those who died are buried in a shallow grave back there." He pointed to the stack of wooden boxes up against the back wall. Bonnie knew there was a door behind those boxes that led to the hospital rooms where they took Grant because Amanda showed it to her. "The spirits of those people who died here were so angry. The only way the spirits could escape is if this building was destroyed. Grant Bellards was the angriest. When Rose's mother passed away from a bad illness and Rose was brought here, Grant was able to learn how to possess his daughter and use her like a puppet to carry out his plan. When he took over her body, he gave Rose the power to carry out the evil deeds that took place here. He thought if enough children got hurt the state would close Firefly Meadows and tear it down."

Bonnie let out a nervous laugh and said, "Well, it looks like nature took care of that! But…why couldn't you tell us yourselves, and why couldn't Amanda just tell me?" Bonnie asked.

"Ah yes, Amanda," their Dad said, "Grant kept a close watch on Amanda's spirit, she wasn't safe. Grant's power was so great that Amanda's soul was in danger even in the ghost world. She could not spend much time communicating with you, Bonnie."

"How do you know all of this, Dad?" Anne asked.

"We have been watching you this whole time, to make sure you two were safe."

Their parents smiled gently.

"So, you two have been *STALKING* us?!" Bonnie asked.

"If you want to put it that way…" Mr. Bleaster laughed.

"Oh, Bonnie!" her Mom said with a smile.

"Mom, Dad, could you tell me where Amanda is? Is she still here? I'd like to see her again," Bonnie begged.

"Outside," their parents said pointed at the door at the top of the stairs, "careful going up, we'll meet you out there."

The glowing doorway and their parents vanished.

"Bonnie, I guess you can let go of my arm now," Anne said still in disbelief.

"Oh yeah, sorry." Bonnie let go of Anne's arm and they headed up the stairs.

When they got to the top of the stairway, they couldn't believe what they saw. Chairs and tables had been thrown way out into the playground. Walls were completely missing. In fact, most of the large stone building was in a million pieces all over the meadow. Fortunately, everyone had made it into the basement and were all right.

Just then, Bonnie noticed a girl with crazy, windswept hair in the distance.

"Anne, it's Amanda! Take my hand!!" Bonnie grabbed Anne's hand and sure enough she could see Amanda waving at them.

"I have to go. Thanks, Bonnie," said Amanda in a warm voice. "Thank you for listening to me."

And just like that, she dissolved into the spring air.

"Bye, Amanda. Thank you for being my friend for a little while."

Tears were already filling Bonnie's eyes when their parents reappeared in front of her and Anne.

"Girls, we have to go, too. We are so sorry about what happened to us."

"What? What happened to you?" Bonnie asked.

"BONNIE!!!" Anne let go of Bonnie's hand which made their parents disappear from Anne's eyes. "THEY ARE DEAD! DO YOU KNOW WHY THEY HAVE A YELLOW OUTLINE? BECAUSE THEY ARE GHOSTS! DO YOU KNOW WHY THEY HAVE BEEN WATCHING US THIS WHOLE TIME? THEY HAVEN'T BEEN STALKING US, THEY HAVE BEEN SPIRITS WATCHING OVER US!" Anne took a deep breath and continued, "Don't get confused, Bonnie. You have a special gift. You can see ghosts. You can see them on the ground walking around like normal people, but that *doesn't* mean they are *alive*."

Bonnie stared in shock at Anne and her eyes started filling with tears. She turned to her parents. They looked sad, nodding in agreement with what Anne had just said. Bonnie grabbed Anne's hand again, knowing that her parents were going to say their last goodbyes.

"Bonnie," said their father with a sad but proud look, "we died in that fire, but we had a purpose to watch over you two. We knew this place was dangerous, but we knew you two could figure things out and make it through…and you did. Our time here is now done."

"We probably won't see you two for a long time," said their Mom, "but we will be waiting. We can't wait to see you both again in the afterlife. Even if you both are old with grey hair, you will still be our little girls."

"I don't want you to go. I don't want you to go…" Bonnie repeated, tears streaming down her face.

"We love you so much, and we're so proud of both of you. Take care of each other," said their Mom.

Anne was crying to where she couldn't talk anymore. She just silently mouthed the words, "I love you..."

Their parents waved goodbye, their bodies turning into smoke as they slowly disappeared into the soft morning breeze.

Anne and Bonnie hugged each other and wept as the scene behind them showed the orphans and staff slowly walking out of the door to the basement. They looked stunned at what they saw as Madame Zoe began to take a head count of all the children. In the distance several police cars and a firetruck could be seen heading toward what was left of Firefly Meadows Orphanage.

# ❧ Epilogue ❧

March 29, 1955, the day of the storm that destroyed Firefly Meadows Orphanage.

The authorities did eventually remove the large, wooden boxes on the wall of the basement and found the hallway of rooms. Back there they found several bodies of the patients who died in a shallow grave.

None of the orphans told anyone the truth about Firefly Meadows, the incident with Rose, stories of ghosts and angry spirits…they let those secrets die with the building.

Anne and Bonnie later got a telegram saying that they actually had a long-lost aunt who finally found out about what happened. She eventually adopted them and they moved to Washington, D.C. They all live in a very nice house, which has a large library, and have been happy ever since.

Rose had no memory of what her father's spirit made her do while he possessed her, she was innocent of everything. A family found out about her through the news of the tornado that destroyed her orphanage. They felt bad for her, especially because she was paralyzed. So, they adopted her and gave her a warm, loving home.

The rest of the orphans moved to a new orphanage in another part of the state. A nicer one, too.

Madame Zoe, Ms. Maria and the rest of the staff soon found different jobs but never saw each other again.

One of early Spring's first days was coming to an end at the ruins of the old orphanage. The meadows looked peaceful as green grass began to grow through the dead weeds and leaves began to grow on the trees. As the sun began to set behind the forest, as the shadows stretched out to the piles of walls and windows, small flashes began to light up all over the fields. Soon, hundreds of fireflies appeared out of the growing darkness like some kind of star shower on earth.

One of the last glimmers of sunlight caught a broken gate that lay on the ground. A sign was still attached to that old gate. A sign that simply read;

## FIREFLY MEADOWS

CPSIA information can be obtained
at www.ICGtesting.com
Printed in the USA
LVHW051931300519
619629LV00011B/21/P